SCAVENGER HUNT

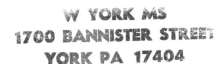

Janet Lorimer

SADDLEBACK
PAGETURNERS
• SPY •

PAGETURNERS

Development and Production: Laurel Associates, Inc.
Cover Illustrator: Black Eagle Productions

SADDLEBACK
EDUCATIONAL PUBLISHING
Three Watson
Irvine, CA 92618-2767
Website: www.sdlback.com

ISBN-10: 1-56254-139-0
ISBN-13: 978-1-56254-139-2
eBook: 978-1-60291-241-0

Printed in the United States of America
11 10 09 08 07   9 8 7 6 5 4 3 2

CONTENTS

Chapter 1

The doorbell rang while Susan Hoskins was grating cheese over a pan of lasagne. "Jay," she called. "Can you get that, please?"

There was no answer. Susan gritted her teeth as she set the cheese aside. Her brother had let her know earlier that he wasn't happy to hear they were having company tonight.

"It's just *your* dumb friend," he'd complained. "It'll be boring."

"You'll like Roger," Susan protested. "He knows a lot about computers."

Jay glared at his sister. "Big deal! So do I. If you'd buy me the software I need . . . " He threw up his arms and stormed out of the room.

The doorbell chimed a second time.

Susan wiped her hands on a dish towel and went to answer it.

Roger was standing in the hall outside the apartment. He was holding a bouquet of roses in one hand and a mysterious-looking box in the other.

"Here," Roger said as he handed her the flowers. "For the lovely hostess."

Susan smiled and buried her nose in the fragrant blossoms. "They're beautiful, Roger," she said. "Thanks."

Roger nodded and looked around. "Where's your brother?" he asked. "I have something for him, too."

"Oh, goody! More flowers?" Jay's voice dripped sarcasm.

Susan turned to see her brother leaning casually against the far wall. She hoped he wouldn't embarrass her tonight. But with Jay she never knew. He was 15 and full of resentment.

Their parents had died when Jay was 10. Susan, 12 years older, had been awarded custody of her kid brother.

She'd been glad they could stay together. At the same time, raising a younger brother was not easy. Susan worked full time and went to college part time. Trying to find enough time to take care of everything—including Jay—was always a challenge.

"You must be Jay." Roger's voice cut across Susan's thoughts. "I hear you're pretty good with computers." He grinned and handed the box to the boy.

Jay just shrugged. "What's this?"

"Why don't you open it and find out?" Roger eyed Jay with amusement.

Susan motioned Roger to sit down as Jay dropped onto the sofa. While he ripped away tape and paper, his brows knotted into a puzzled frown. But then Jay realized what he was holding. "It can't be!" he whooped.

"What is it?" Susan asked.

"Lion of Destiny." Jay's voice dropped to a near whisper. He gazed at Roger as if the man had just handed him the keys

to a gleaming, brand new Porsche.

"Excuse me?" Susan gazed from one guy to the other. They seemed to be communicating in some strange way that left her out.

Roger's grin widened. "*Lion of Destiny* is a new computer game," he said. "It's the hottest thing on the market."

Susan's jaw dropped. "Roger, I know you can't afford—"

"Dumpster diving," he said proudly. "I think it was probably a mistake on the part of some college kid—but you never know. Still, the software *was* abandoned. That and a TV in perfect condition, a couple of speakers, a—"

"Abandoned?" Jay howled. "Did you say that someone *threw away* this brand-new game? Where?"

"In a dumpster," Roger said with a laugh. "Do you mean your sister hasn't told you about my hobby?"

Jay gazed from Roger to Susan. "You never said—"

"You never listen," she snapped. "Remember? You said you didn't want to hear about my co-workers because they were all so old and boring."

Jay turned three shades of red. Susan knew that later, after Roger left, Jay would probably jump down her throat for saying that. But right now—

Roger burst out laughing. "*Old*, huh? Hey, I'm not even 30, Jay. But I guess that qualifies as old if—"

"Tell me about the software," Jay interrupted. "Where did you find it?"

"I told you, in a dumpster." Roger shrugged off the jacket he was wearing. As Susan took it, she noticed that Jay cast an envious look at the jacket. Although it wasn't new, it was leather. Jay would have given a year's worth of fast food meals for a leather jacket. Roger saw the look, too. "Same goes for the jacket," he said off-handedly.

Jay straightened up as if someone had poured hot lead down his spine.

"No way! You *found* that jacket?"

"Yeah, I sure did—in a dumpster," Roger said, nodding.

Susan hung up Roger's jacket and headed for the kitchen. She heard her friend say, "Yeah, Jay, I'm a dumpster diver. Do you know what that is, man? It's someone who crawls through trash to find treasure. I've really got some great stories—"

As Susan slid the pan of lasagne into the oven, she wondered if inviting Roger to dinner had been such a good idea. The *last* thing she wanted was for Jay to become a dumpster diver.

Chapter 2

"So there I was—at the end of an alley with a security guard the size of a tank coming at me. No way out!" Roger paused for dramatic effect.

Jay's plate of delicious lasagne went unnoticed. "Then what happened?"

"I pulled an old trick," Roger said with a grin. "Lucky for me, the guard fell for it. I waited until he was just a few feet away. Then I glanced to the side and cried out, 'Joe, don't do it!' The guard looked away, and I took off. As I whizzed by, he tried to grab me—but it was too late."

Roger and Jay both laughed.

Susan stood up and began to collect the dirty dishes. Roger smiled up at her. "That was really a great dinner, Susan.

Anything I can do to help you out?"

"Stop filling my brother's head with fantastic tales of dumpster diving," she said. Her smile was chilly and she felt a certain amount of pleasure when Roger winced.

"I like Roger's stories," Jay exclaimed. "Come on, Sue. Quit acting like I'm some dumb little kid."

"I'm sorry," Susan said, "but I don't want you thinking that Roger's hobby is all fun and games."

Jay was about to snap back when Roger cut in. "Your sister is right, Jay," he said solemnly. "I can also tell you some stories that would scare you to death. Dumpster diving isn't for kids."

Jay sighed. "I'm not a kid, Roger. So tell me *everything*. What else have you found in dumpsters?"

Roger began reeling off a list of finds. Even Susan was amazed. Roger had found everything from furniture to clothes to electronics to books and more.

"I got started when I was in college," he explained. "I was working my way through school. Money wasn't easy to come by back then. I found that I could survive amazingly well with stuff I found in trash bins. At the end of each semester, for example, students toss out a lot of supplies. I'd find paper, pens, pencils—all good enough to use."

Susan frowned and shook her head. "How wasteful!"

"If you think that's bad," Roger went on, "you should see what else people throw away. How about perfectly good food? I found unopened packages and cans just tossed out with the garbage."

Susan shuddered. "I don't think I'd encourage anyone to eat food from a dumpster," she said.

"Neither would I," Roger said, "but the point I'm making is that we live in a very wasteful society."

"Maybe I'm just old-fashioned," Susan said, "but don't you think it's a crime to waste so much?"

"Absolutely," Roger said. "But I don't have a solution, Susan."

"Think about it, Sue. That's what makes dumpster diving a good thing," Jay said. "Don't you see? It keeps stuff from going to waste."

"Remember, one person's trash is another person's treasure," Roger said. "Some of the stuff I've found is definitely treasure."

"Well, I see your point," Susan said, "but I still think it's far too dangerous." She picked up the stack of plates and headed for the kitchen.

"It can be very dangerous," she heard Roger say. "You have to know what you're doing, what the laws are."

Susan began to scrape the plates. As she did, she took a good look at what she was throwing out. It was the first time she had really thought about it.

"There are three important things to remember," she heard Roger say. "First, you need to know what the laws are in this town. In some cities, it's against the law to go through trash cans. In other places, trash on the curb is considered abandoned property. Second, don't trespass. That means you can't search a dumpster on private property. And last, don't steal. But that's just common sense, of course."

"Cool," Jay said. "Now tell me just exactly where you found the *Lion of Destiny* disks."

Susan recognized the excitement in his voice. She didn't like the sound of it.

Chapter 3

Susan woke up with a start. For a moment she stared up at the ceiling, listening. Had a sound awakened her? She heard nothing now. She glanced at the clock. Not quite five. *Five?* But it was a Saturday morning. Why had she awakened?

She turned over and tried to go back to sleep. She stretched and pounded her pillow just right, but she was too wide-awake. At last she got up.

On her way to the kitchen, she stopped outside Jay's door. How odd. He usually slept with his bedroom door closed. This morning it was partly open.

Susan tapped lightly on the doorframe, then pushed the door all the way open and looked in. She couldn't believe her eyes—Jay's bed was empty!

"Jay?" Susan called out. *"Jay?"* No answer. Maybe he was in the bathroom. Or the kitchen. Or—

Susan quickly searched through the apartment. Her brother was gone! She looked for a note, but didn't find one. It wasn't like Jay to go off without leaving a note. And it certainly wasn't like him to go out this early—especially on a Saturday. On weekends, Jay always clung to his pillow as long as he could.

Susan collapsed onto her brother's unmade bed and gazed around the room. She tried to steady her nerves.

"Think!" she told herself. "Where would he have gone? And why would he leave the house so early?"

Memories of Jay's conversation with Roger came back to her. After dinner, she had tried to get a game of Scrabble going, but Jay was having none of it. All he wanted to do was talk to Roger about dumpster diving!

Susan groaned as she thought back. What had Jay wanted to know? He had asked where to dive for computer software and hardware. What the risks were. How to dress. What to look out for. Susan remembered Jay's face. He had hung onto every word that Roger had uttered.

After Roger left, Susan had reminded her brother that it was his turn to wash the dishes. Oddly enough, he hadn't put up much of a struggle. A little later she'd carried the dessert plates to the kitchen. That was when she'd seen Jay talking on the phone with one of his friends. She hadn't listened in. Living in a small apartment, they'd agreed to respect each other's privacy. But she remembered now that Jay had acted funny—like a little kid caught in the act of doing something wrong!

Susan's mouth tightened in anger. "Thanks a lot, Roger," she thought.

Outside, Susan heard the roaring

engine of a trash-collecting truck. She glanced at the clock. It was almost 5:30. The sun was coming up. If Jay had gone diving, he should have been home hours before the trucks made their rounds.

Something must be wrong! Susan knew it was silly for her to worry so much about Jay—but she couldn't help it. And she couldn't just sit there and wait for him to show up. It was time to share the worry with someone else— *Roger!* As far as Susan was concerned, Roger was responsible. Why shouldn't he help her find her brother? Besides, he'd know where to look.

Susan hurried to the kitchen and dialed Roger's number. The phone rang again and again. When Roger finally answered, she felt a certain satisfaction, knowing that she'd awakened him.

When she outlined her problem, Roger woke up fast. "Are you *sure* he went diving?" he asked.

"As sure as I can be," she snapped.

"Think about it, Roger. He's 15 and this is a Saturday. How likely is it that he's studying at the library?"

"Oh, he can't be. The library in your neighborhood won't open until—" Roger stopped, embarrassed. Then he chuckled uncomfortably. "Okay, I see your point. How likely is it that he went to spend the night with a pal?"

"If Jay wanted to sleep over at a friend's house, he would have told me," Susan said. "At the very least, he would have left a note."

"Okay, okay," Roger said. "I'll get dressed and go look—"

"Not without me," Susan cut in. "Pick me up in 20 minutes, Roger. I'll be waiting right here." She hung up before he could say no.

Chapter 4

A loud banging on the front door surprised Susan. It couldn't be Roger already. She opened the door with a glad cry, thinking it was Jay.

Roger stood in the hall, gazing at her with a puzzled frown. Given his rumpled look, Susan wondered if he'd gotten dressed while he drove. He pushed past her into the apartment.

"So he's not back yet?" Roger asked, his glance darting around the small living room.

"No," Susan said. "I already called two of his friends. Jay wasn't with them. When I phoned his best friend, there was no answer. It's possible the two boys might have gone diving together. Jay was so intrigued by your stories—"

"Now wait a minute," Roger said defensively. "Don't blame me! The kids might have taken off to see a movie or gone to play pool or—"

Susan crossed her arms and gazed at Roger. "In the middle of the night? Fat chance. I can tell you don't know a lot about teenagers," she said. "Jay was fascinated by the idea of finding more computer games for free."

"Oh, but that was just pure luck," Roger sputtered. "The chances of that happening again—"

"I know, but *Jay* doesn't realize that," Susan explained. "He imagines he's going to reach into any old dumpster and pull out gold!"

Roger sighed. "Okay. Maybe I did get a little carried away with some of my stories. But come on, Susan! Let's not waste time by standing around here arguing. Let's go find the kid!"

As they climbed into the car, Susan said, "Last night you gave Jay a list of places where you've found software. Remember?"

Roger nodded. "Most of the best places are around companies that *make* game software. Sometimes they get rid of the out-of-date stuff to make way for new software."

"Is that where we're going? To one of those companies?"

Roger pulled onto the street. "It's as good a place as any to start. But there's one thing I don't understand. If the kids *did* go diving—where are they now? They can't be hanging out by a dumpster now. It's daylight! The trucks have already made their rounds and picked up the trash. Why would the kids still be—"

"What if one of the boys got hurt?" Susan asked in agony. It was a fear she had not wanted to put into words.

"Then the other one would have gone for help," Roger said. "Is that it? Are you afraid that Jay got hurt and his friend just took off? Left him there?"

Susan sighed. "Buddy means well, but he never struck me as being a very responsible kid," she said.

Roger cast a doubtful glance in her direction. "Maybe, but, Susan—the kid is Jay's best friend."

Susan groaned and sank back against the seat. "Maybe I'm wrong. Jay says I'm too hard on him and his friends. But it isn't easy trying to be mother and father to a teenager."

"Relax," Roger said. "We're here."

"Here" was an alley that ran for several blocks behind a long line of businesses. The companies in this office park made everything from computer hardware to software, from CD players to cell phones.

Roger slowed at the mouth of the alley. "You keep an eye out for Jay," he said. "Something else you should know. Some of these places keep the dumpsters close to the alley. The parking area is fenced in and security guards patrol the property. If the dumpster is *outside* the fence, it's fair game."

Susan nodded impatiently. She remembered what Roger had said about dumpster diving and the law.

"But some businesses keep their dumpsters *inside* the fence," Roger went on. "That means their dumpsters are on private property. They don't want anyone going through their trash. If Jay climbed a fence to get into one of those dumpsters, he broke the law."

Roger looked at Susan to see if she really understood what he was saying. "And they might have been caught?" she asked nervously. "Are you saying we should go to the police?"

"If we don't find Jay, that would be the next step," Roger said slowly. "And I'm afraid that some of these guards can get pretty heavy-handed—even with a kid. If worst comes to worst, we should check the hospitals."

Chapter 5

Roger drove slowly down the alley. All of a sudden, Susan spotted a couple of police cars. They were parked at the far end; the lights on top were flashing.

"They're parked by the HyperPlay building," Roger muttered. "HyperPlay makes computer games."

"Like *Lion of Destiny*?" Susan asked.

"Exactly. They keep their dumpsters *inside* the fence. All the divers know that's a place to stay away from."

"You don't suppose—" Susan started to say. She couldn't keep the dread out of her voice.

"Don't worry, I know the guard," Roger said. "Hang on."

He pulled to the side, parked, and got out. Susan watched him saunter across the street and start a conversation with a security guard.

As they talked, she glanced around. She and Roger were not the only onlookers. A small crowd of curiosity seekers had been drawn to the site. Susan saw several people who looked like they might be homeless. She spotted a jogger, still running in place. A few workers leaned against the fence on the opposite side of the alley.

Susan wondered if the workers had come out of the HyperPlay building. Maybe they had just come off a late night shift. Two women and a man talked as they watched the police.

One of the workers seemed to look directly at Susan. She dropped her gaze. For some reason, she felt guilty. It was as if the words *Thief's Sister* had been stamped on her forehead.

At that moment, Roger returned. He started the car and said, "The guard told me a couple of kids went through the company's dumpster last night. When they were spotted, they took off. But they were carrying something with them. That's why the cops were called in."

Susan put her head in her hands. "Jay and Buddy?"

Roger shrugged. "Don't know. Look, just to be on the safe side, let's keep searching. I'll drive by those condos near the college."

He pulled out of the alley and turned onto the street. "You'd be amazed by what students toss out when the semester is over," he said. "One day they wake up to find that finals are over and so are those end-of-the-semester parties. And their lease is up, too!"

"So the students just throw out their belongings?" Susan remarked.

"Oh, they pack as much as they can into their cars. But the rest gets left behind," Roger said.

Susan shook her head. "Tell me something. Did you find that *Lion of*

Destiny game near the college?"

Roger nodded. "Maybe someone tossed the game out by accident. On the other hand, some people just *have* to own the most up-to-date stuff!"

But their search turned up nothing. Finally, Roger suggested that Susan call her apartment. "Maybe your brother came home after we left," he said. "Here, use my cell phone."

There was no answer. Susan's vague worry began to congeal into hard, cold fear. She knew there were a lot of places they hadn't looked. And she supposed there must be other explanations for Jay's disappearance. But she was still frightened.

"Let's go back to your place," Roger said. He glanced at Susan's hands, knotted tightly in her lap. "It's not quite eight. Still early. I'll bet you that Jay will be home any minute now."

When they unlocked the door of Susan's apartment, Roger begged her to make him some breakfast. "My stomach is growling. I'm so hungry I could eat your couch!" he cried with a comic moan.

Susan smiled. She suspected that Roger was trying to keep her mind off her brother. And by now Susan was hungry, too. A few minutes later, she was carrying a plate of scrambled eggs to the table when the front door burst open. There stood Jay!

Chapter 6

Susan was so happy to see Jay that she almost dropped the plate. Roger grabbed it just as she threw her arms around her brother. But she quickly drew back with a choking sound of disgust. "You *stink*!" she cried out.

Jay laughed. "Yeah, I know. Buddy and I got into some rank places."

He started for the table, but Roger reached out and stopped him. Susan had never seen Roger look so serious.

"Go clean up, Jay," Roger said. "Then we're going to have a little talk about what you did."

Jay grinned sheepishly. "I figured you'd be mad. But when I tell you guys what we found—"

Roger held up his hand. "First tell

me where you were. Did you dive in a HyperPlay dumpster?" he asked.

Jay nodded. "How'd you know?"

"The cops are looking for you and Buddy right now," Roger said sternly. "What were you thinking of? I warned you about the law. Didn't I tell you *never* to dive in a dumpster on private property and—"

"I know, I know, but HyperPlay makes the coolest—"

"Don't interrupt!" Roger roared. Jay stared at the man in shock.

"Good!" Susan thought. "A harsh scolding is just what Jay needs."

"It doesn't matter what HyperPlay makes," Roger continued in a calmer tone. "You boys trespassed on private property. The security guard said you stole something from the dumpster. That means *you broke the law!*"

Jay's face turned pale.

"If you and your friend are smart," Roger said carefully, "you'll turn yourselves in. You'll tell the cops you didn't know you were breaking the law. You'll apologize. Then you'll turn in whatever you took from the dumpster and—" Roger paused. "By the way, what *did* you take?"

The color returned to Jay's cheeks. He grinned excitedly. "It looks like another *Lion of Destiny* game—but even better. This one seems to be a real early version. It's called *Lion of Doom*."

"Where is it?" Roger demanded.

"Buddy's got it," Jay explained. "He wanted to load it on his computer while I went home to get cleaned up. Then Buddy's going to—"

At that moment the phone rang. Susan jumped off the couch and ran to the kitchen. She answered it and held up the receiver. "Jay? It's Buddy. He says he needs to talk to you right away."

"Cool!" Jay started for the kitchen, but Roger grabbed the boy's arm.

"Listen, you," Roger said. "Tell

Buddy that under no circumstances is he to copy that disk. You hear?"

Jay's smile vanished. "Why not? We have an advance copy of *Lion of Doom*."

"And if HyperPlay presses charges, you both could end up going to jail," Roger snapped. "You just don't get how serious this is, do you?"

Roger rolled his eyes and looked at Susan. His expression seemed to say, "Help me, for crying out loud!"

Susan smiled at her friend and shrugged her shoulders. Roger was right. Jay actually didn't seem to have a clue about how serious his crime was.

Jay got on the phone with Buddy and started to talk. Susan watched as his excitement quickly faded. "You did it wrong, Buddy. You must have. You—" Jay's frown deepened. He listened again. Then he told Buddy to bring the disk to the apartment. When he hung up, Jay looked very annoyed.

"What's wrong?" Susan said.

"Buddy says there's something wrong with the disk. He says it's not *Lion of Doom* after all. It starts out that way—but then it becomes something else." Jay ran his hand through his hair and sighed in exasperation. "Buddy's stupid. He probably messed it up."

"You'd better hope not," Roger said. "Go on now and get cleaned up."

As the boy disappeared into the bathroom, Roger turned back to his scrambled eggs. Susan joined him. In spite of her worry, the excitement of the morning had given her an appetite, too.

Susan was scrambling more eggs when Buddy arrived. She introduced him to Roger. But instead of shaking hands, Buddy slapped the disk onto the table. "Here! It's just a bunch of junk." Buddy sounded disgusted.

Jay grabbed the disk. "You probably did something wrong, Buddy," he grumbled impatiently.

"Ha! I know more about computers

than *you* do," Buddy snorted.

Roger put a stop to their bickering by grabbing the disk back. "Okay, let's take a look at it and see what you've got," he said. "That'll make everybody happy."

They all trooped into Jay's room. Roger sat down at the computer and turned it on. Susan hovered behind them until she remembered the eggs. She was in the kitchen when she heard Jay's cry of anguish and the exclamations of anger from Roger and Buddy.

She ran to the bedroom door. "What happened?" she asked.

Roger turned to explain. The look on his face startled her. "Something is very wrong with this disk," he exclaimed. "We just crashed Jay's computer!"

Chapter 7

For a while, Susan wondered what the neighbors must think. Jay and Buddy were yelling at the top of their lungs about which boy was to blame. And Roger was trying to calm them down by yelling even louder.

Susan finally got their attention when she yelled, "*Cops!*"

Roger, Buddy, and Jay turned and gazed at her in silent horror. Susan took a deep breath. "If you don't quiet down, we'll have the cops knocking on our door," she said in a normal voice.

"Susan is right," Roger told the boys. "Stop yelling and listen to me." He turned to Buddy. "Is this what happened to your computer? Did it act like this after you loaded the game?"

Buddy nodded. Roger sighed. When he spoke again, it was to both boys. "This disk you found is infected with a virus. I can get rid of the virus and clean up your computers. But you guys are going to lose a lot of stuff. I just hope you've kept your files backed up."

The boys glanced at each other. From their horrified expressions, Susan could tell they had not. She sighed. It was a hard lesson to learn, but one they wouldn't forget.

"Wait a minute," Buddy said. "How did the disk get infected?"

"Interesting question," Roger said. "I think we've got a big problem on our hands." He turned to Jay. "When you found the disk, was it just lying by itself—a loose disk?"

Jay shook his head. "No, it was in a package. That was what made it so neat! It looked like brand-new software they'd just thrown away."

Roger thought about that for a

minute. It wasn't right. "I don't like the sound of this," he said.

"Why not?" Jay argued. "Come on, Roger! You said that's how you found my *Lion of Destiny* game."

"Not exactly," Roger said. "First of all, I found that game in a dumpster near the college condos. It was across town in a different kind of dumpster. Second, I didn't have to trespass to get to the dumpster. That should have told you something right from the start."

Roger headed for the living room with Susan and the boys trailing behind. He dropped onto the sofa, his brows knit in a puzzled frown. Jay, Buddy, and Susan watched him quietly.

"HyperPlay keeps its dumpsters on private property for a good reason," Roger said slowly. "In fact, their trash is carried away by a private company instead of the city trash collectors. That's their insurance. If a game *does* get dumped, no one else can get a copy."

"Yeah? So what?" Jay cried out impatiently. "What about the virus?"

Roger flashed a look of annoyance at Jay. "Can you hold on for a moment?" he snapped. Jay looked disgusted, but he kept quiet.

"When I loaded the disk," Roger said to Susan, "it started out the way *Lion of Destiny* starts. Anyone would think it was a normal game. But after just a few minutes of play, the virus took over."

"That almost sounds like it was done on purpose," Susan said. "Who would do that? It makes no sense."

"Right. I think it must be deliberate," Roger said. "That's what bothers me. HyperPlay has built up a rock-solid reputation for creating wonderful, problem-free games."

"So what's the deal with the virus?" Buddy asked with a puzzled look. "Why would they sabotage their own games? Why would anybody ruin—"

"That's the point," Roger said.

"But if they packaged it to look like the others," Susan said, "they must have intended it to be sold in the store. And that means—" She drew her breath in sharply. "Oh, I see. Good grief, Roger! The company would be ruined."

He nodded. "Of course. Imagine what would happen if someone created these infected disks on a grand scale. What if they flooded the market with infected *Lion of Doom* disks at the very same time the company announced its new *Lion of Doom* game? People who liked the *Destiny* game would be sure to snatch up the *Doom* sequel. And everybody who accidentally bought the infected disks would crash their computers. Then there would be an investigation, and a giant recall—and HyperPlay would very likely go under."

Susan looked confused. "But who would want to do something like that?" she exclaimed. "I don't understand. Why deliberately ruin the company?"

Roger's eyes narrowed as he thought it through. Then he said, "Back in 1988, a computer programmer was convicted of wiping out more than 160,000 payroll records with a computer virus. He'd been fired from an insurance company, so he planted the virus in revenge."

"I get the picture. You think it's an unhappy employee," Susan said. "But if HyperPlay has such tight security, how could an ex-employee get back inside to plant the phony disk? And how did the infected disk end up in the dumpster?"

"Maybe it *isn't* someone who was fired," Jay said slowly. "Maybe it's just an unhappy worker."

Roger nodded. "That makes a lot more sense. It could be someone who's been warned about making too many mistakes. Or maybe it's someone who called in sick too often."

"Or someone who didn't get a raise or a promotion," Susan suggested.

Roger nodded. "As for how the disk

got in the dumpster, there are several possibilities. It *could* have been an accident. The important thing is to find out who created the virus. And that had better happen *right now*—before he or she creates more infected disks and ruins the company."

"And just who is going to do that?" Susan asked.

All three of the guys were staring at *her*.

Chapter 8

Susan looked at Roger nervously. "You're joking, right?" she burst out.

Roger shook his head. Then Jay said, "Hey, what are we thinking of, guys? My sister couldn't find a rattlesnake if she sat on it."

"Thanks a lot!" Susan exclaimed. "Roger, this isn't funny. *We* shouldn't do anything except call the police. We can tell them what the boys did and what we found on the disk. Then we'll let the cops take it from there."

"Aren't you forgetting that Buddy and Jay are already in trouble with the cops?" Roger said.

"No," Susan said worriedly. "I haven't forgotten. But—"

"What if the cops suspect that the

boys *created* the virus?" Roger went on.

"That's ridiculous!" Susan glared at Roger. "Give me a break. You're turning this whole thing into—"

Jay put his hand on his sister's arm. "Listen to him, Susan. Roger could be right," he said.

Susan glanced at her brother in surprise. "But why would the cops think such a thing?" she asked.

"Because people *do* create computer viruses—just for the fun of it," Jay said. "Some guys get a kick out of seeing other people suffer."

"Whoever created the virus would quickly find out the cops have the disk and be warned off. Then he or she would be free to create another infected disk," Roger said.

Susan couldn't argue with that. "But if we can't go to the cops, what *are* we going to do?" she said.

"Hold on, Susan. I've got a plan," Roger said. "But first I have to make a couple of calls. Be back in a minute."

When he came back from the kitchen, he said, "I called a friend of mine who keeps up with the computer game industry. I didn't tell him what was going on. I just asked about *Lion of Doom*. Apparently, all the insiders have heard about the new game. It's supposed to be released soon."

Susan groaned. "I thought *Lion of Destiny* was the hot new item," she said.

"It was," Roger said with a laugh. "But sales are slowing. In the world of computers, things move very fast, Susan. What's hot today is cold tomorrow. *Lion of Doom* will skyrocket sales."

"So what do we do now?" Buddy asked impatiently.

Roger didn't answer. Susan glanced over at him and saw that he was studying her closely. Suddenly, she had a cold feeling of dread right in the pit of her stomach.

"Every time that question comes up,

you look at *me*!" she cried. "So let's hear it—what's on your mind, Roger?"

"We need to get someone inside HyperPlay," Roger said. "Someone who can do a little snooping."

Susan's eyes widened. "But *I'm* not a spy!" she burst out. "Besides, I already have a perfectly good job, remember?"

"But you've got some vacation time coming, don't you?" Roger said. "You can apply for a temporary job. It won't take long to find out what we need to know. It's the only way we can get the boys off the hook."

"But I don't know *anything* about computer games, Roger! Besides—there may not even be a job opening at HyperPlay. Not even for a temp worker. Then what?"

"HyperPlay is growing fast," Roger said. "They've been advertising in the paper for part-time workers."

Susan stared at Roger in disbelief. Jay's prank was becoming a nightmare.

Chapter 9

Susan glanced at the clock on the wall. On Saturday morning, Roger had cooked up this crazy scheme. Now it was Monday, 10:00 in the morning. Susan was sitting in HyperPlay's personnel office being interviewed for a job.

"When I think of what a great vacation I had planned," she thought bitterly. "Instead, here I am—"

The interviewer looked up from her application. Susan tried to look eager. The interviewer smiled. "How do you feel about shift work?"

Half an hour later, Susan left the HyperPlay building. She crossed the street, walked to the corner, and waited for the light. Roger was waiting for her in a coffee shop just down the block.

As she stepped off the curb, she saw several people walking toward her. One of them—a tall young man—looked vaguely familiar to her. While she was trying to remember where she'd seen him, she had another thought.

"What if I run into someone I know at HyperPlay? How could I explain what I'm doing there?" she wondered silently. As she passed by the cluster of people, she dropped her gaze. But she had a funny feeling that at least one person in the group was staring at her.

Inside the coffee shop, Susan quickly spotted Roger. She slid across the plastic seat of the booth where he was sitting.

"I got the job!" She smiled broadly. "Of course it's just an entry-level no-brainer—but at least I'm in."

"Good for you," Roger said. "I knew you could do it." He signaled the waitress. "Now we have to talk about what you're going to look for."

That evening Susan reported for

work at HyperPlay. Her shift began at 6:00. Most of the employees had already left for the day. Only a small crew was kept on at night.

As soon as Susan clocked in, she was given her first task. "I need this stack of paperwork filed," said Mrs. Kelly, the night shift supervisor.

Susan nodded.

"Funny thing about computers," Mrs. Kelly grumbled. "They keep telling us we'll have less paperwork. So far, I sure haven't found that to be true!"

Susan laughed and scooped up the stack of folders.

Mrs. Kelly kept an eye on her for a couple of minutes. When she was sure that Susan knew exactly what to do, she relaxed. "I'm going across the street for a cup of coffee," the woman said.

Alone now, Susan hunted for the personnel files. She had a feeling they'd be locked up, and she wasn't wrong. But luckily, Roger had taught her how to break into a locked file cabinet.

"Like brother, like sister, I suppose," she'd grumbled as she tried it out a few times. "I can't believe that I'm practicing to become a full-fledged criminal."

"It's all for a good cause," Roger had grinned. "And it might be helpful if you thought of yourself as a secret agent instead of a criminal."

Susan looked around. Then she slipped the small screwdriver out of her pocket and went to work. It was going to take time to search the personnel files for records of unhappy employees. If her boss took a half-hour break, she'd get through *some* of the files—but not all in one night. It looked like she was going to be working at this job for a while. Susan reached for the first file and started to read.

Chapter 10

It took several nights, but before the end of the week, Susan had a list of suspects. On Thursday afternoon, before she started work, she met Roger across the street at the coffee shop.

"After tonight, I don't think we should meet here," Roger said. "Some of your new friends might wonder who I am. Better if we aren't seen together."

"Ha! *What* new friends?" Susan demanded. "I don't have time to make friends, Roger."

"Oh, yeah?" Roger grinned. "What about that group that just walked in?"

Susan glanced over her shoulder. It was the same group she saw every evening. It seemed that they, too, worked the night shift. She hadn't actually been introduced, but she always greeted them with a smile and they smiled back.

Tonight, Susan looked quickly away. Again, as on Monday, she had a funny feeling that she knew a couple of them. She worried that they might be people who knew her from her full-time job. Or they might recognize her from one of the college classes she was taking.

"Relax," Roger muttered. "You look as if you're guilty of something."

"No kidding. What about breaking and entering?" she hissed.

Roger grinned and began to softly whistle the theme from the James Bond movies. Susan groaned. "*Pssst, ya got da list, babe?*" he hissed out of the corner of his mouth.

Susan could have smacked him with the envelope she was carrying. But instead, she slid it across the table. Roger opened it and pulled out a stack of pages. Susan had photocopied the files of the employees she had suspected.

Roger quickly scanned the pages. "Looks like we have three possible suspects," he said quietly. "Let's see— Andy Walker, Jane Burkhart, and Patricia Leong."

"Jane Burkhart seems to have the strongest motive," Susan whispered. She kept glancing around nervously, hoping that no one could overhear what they were saying.

"What makes you say that?" Roger looked up in surprise.

"Because she's been disciplined several times for being late for work and for having a poor attitude," Susan said. "And I gather she talks back to her boss a lot. Not a good way to make friends and influence people."

"That's true," Roger frowned as he glanced from one file to the next. "But on the other hand, look at this guy. Andy Walker was passed over for a promotion twice. He may have a lot of resentment. After all, he's been stuck at the same pay rate for a long time."

"Okay," Susan said, nodding. "What about Patricia Leong? Can we get rid of her as a suspect?"

Roger shook his head. "Doesn't look like it. She was recently criticized a couple of times for sloppy work and—" He frowned and kept on reading. "Her boss even suspected her of passing company secrets to a rival."

"That's serious stuff. Why didn't they fire her?" Susan asked.

"No real proof," Roger said. "Still, this doesn't make her look at all good." He shoved the papers back in the envelope and gazed at the wall as if lost in thought. Then he asked, "Have you met any of these people? Do you know where their cubicles are?"

Susan shook her head. "So far I've been stuck in the business office. Tracking down the suspects in person is my next step," she said.

She got her chance later that evening. Mrs. Kelly asked her to distribute the mail. "They were short-handed this morning," the woman complained. "Seems they didn't have a chance to get all the mail delivered. I know you're new here, Susan, but do your best."

Susan took her time wheeling the mail cart up and down the aisles between the workers' cubicles. Most of the cubicles were empty. The handful of workers who handled this shift seemed to be a relaxed bunch. Most were willing to talk to her and answer her questions.

When she reached Andy Walker's workstation, Susan pulled out a batch of envelopes. The cubicle was empty. Maybe the man had gone to get a cup of coffee, Susan thought.

She was about to stack the letters on his desk when her hand accidentally hit the mouse. The screensaver disappeared and she saw a page of text. To her horror, Susan realized that she was looking at a copy of the virus program!

Susan blinked, unable to believe her eyes. "I must be wrong," she thought wildly. "It *can't* be this easy!"

Then, just at that moment, she felt a hand on her shoulder. "Can I help you?" The voice—so close behind her—made her jump. She whirled around and found herself face-to-face with Andy Walker.

# Chapter 11

"Oh!" Susan exclaimed in a squeaky voice. "You startled me!"

Andy didn't smile. He just repeated his question. "Can I help you?"

Susan forced herself to smile. "I, uh—was just delivering your mail," she said nervously. "I—I'm afraid that my hand accidentally hit the mouse. I—I hope I didn't damage anything."

Andy glanced at the screen. Susan saw a flicker of emotion in his eyes. Then his glance met hers again. He was studying her, as if trying to figure out what she was thinking. "No," he said at last. "It seems to be fine."

"I—I'd better get going, then," Susan stammered. "I have more deliveries to make." She nodded at the cart in the aisle. It was still piled high with mail.

But Andy stood blocking her way, staring at her. "I've seen you around," he said at last. "You're new here, aren't you?"

Susan nodded. "Yes, that's right. I just started work here. I—I'm still learning my way around." She laughed nervously, but her mind was racing.

As she looked at the man, she recalled seeing him outside the building. And she'd seen him somewhere else— but where? While she introduced herself, she struggled to remember. Oh, yes, it was in the coffee shop. But there was somewhere else—

"Guess I'd better let you get back to work," Andy said. He stood aside. Susan thanked him and hurried down the corridor with her mail cart. She finished delivering the rest of the mail as quickly as she could. Then she hurried back to the business office.

Luckily, her boss was out of the office. Susan grabbed the phone and dialed Roger's number. He answered on the second ring. "Roger, I've found him," she whispered hoarsely.

She quickly told him what had happened. "I didn't think it would be this easy," she ended up. "Now what? Do I call the cops, or do you?"

"Hold on, Susan. I'm not sure if it's the cops we want or—"

At that moment Susan heard her boss come in the door and plop her purse down on her desk. "I have to go," she whispered. "Figure out what we should do next and call me."

Susan didn't want to answer Mrs. Kelly's questions about the phone call. So instead of hanging up, she pretended to be listening. "Okay, ten minutes—then you'd better get to bed," she said. But as she started to hang up, Susan heard another sound on the line. Someone else hung up just before she did!

Susan had no time to think about that. She looked up and saw her boss walking toward her. Susan smiled at her. "Hi. I was just checking on my brother. I hope that's okay."

Mrs. Kelly nodded. Susan went back to work typing several reports. An hour later, the phone rang again. It was Roger. "Can you meet me at the coffee shop?" he asked.

"My break is coming up in a few minutes," Susan said. "I'll meet you then."

About 15 minutes later, she slid into Roger's favorite booth at the back of the coffee shop. From there he could see around the restaurant. Susan wondered if he wasn't taking this spy business a little too seriously.

"Okay," she said after she'd ordered, "I hope you have a solution to our problem, Secret Agent Man."

"Very funny." He made a face. "Now, tell me again how you found the guy. Tell me everything he said and what you said. Don't leave anything out."

Susan took a deep breath. Slowly, with as much detail as possible, she told him about how she'd found the program. "Good thing you showed me what it would look like and not just what it would do," she said.

"How did Andy act when he found you in his cubicle?" Roger asked. When Susan told him, he frowned. "Not good. I'm worried that he might suspect you. It sounds like he was pretty nervous."

"I was a nervous wreck myself," Susan said. "I don't know how nervous he was. But I did think he seemed a bit suspicious of me."

"That's what I was afraid of," Roger said. "I've been doing a lot of thinking. I also phoned a few friends in the industry. They believe that our best bet is to take the disk and Jay to the police and tell them the whole story."

"That's what *I've* wanted to do from the beginning," Susan said crossly. "First thing tomorrow—"

"I don't think we should wait that long," Roger said. "If Andy is suspicious, he might just destroy all the proof."

"Are you saying we have to go to the cops *tonight*?"

Roger nodded. "Just as soon as you finish your pie. In the meantime, I'm going to call Jay and tell him to—"

At that moment their waitress came walking up to their booth. "Are you Susan Hoskins? There's a phone call for you."

Susan frowned. "What? Who would be calling me here?"

"Might be your brother," Roger said. "Maybe he called HyperPlay first, and they told him where to find you."

Susan climbed out of the booth and headed for the counter. She picked up the receiver. But it wasn't Jay. She had never heard this voice before. For one thing, the voice was electronically disguised. Susan couldn't even tell if the caller was a man or a woman.

"*If you do not do exactly what I say, you will never see your brother again*," the voice began. Then it told her just what to do.

# Chapter 12

Later, Susan couldn't recall how she had made it back to the booth. Roger took one look at her face and knew that something was wrong. When she told him what the caller had said, Roger's eyes widened. "Jay? *Kidnapped?*"

"Keep your voice down," Susan said. She was shaking from head to toe. "The kidnapper says I have to turn the disk Jay found over to—to *him* and—"

"Wait a minute, Susan!" Roger's eyes narrowed. "You said you couldn't tell if the kidnapper was a man or a woman."

Susan had already told him about the electronically disguised voice. "Come on, Roger! It *has* to be Andy Walker, doesn't it?" she asked.

Roger shook his head. "Walker came

in here about ten minutes ago, got a cup of coffee to go, and took off."

Susan frowned. "But that makes no sense at all. There are coffeepots in the employees' lunchroom. If all he wanted was coffee, why come here?"

Roger shrugged.

"And if Andy Walker came in here while I was on the phone—who called me?" Susan mused. "And from where?"

"Call home," Roger suggested. "Check on Jay. Maybe it's just a hoax."

He handed Susan his cell phone. She tapped in the number, but then waited, shaking her head at Roger's questioning look. "No answer."

"Maybe Jay went to a friend's—"

Susan scrambled out of the booth. "*Maybe* doesn't cut it, Roger. If my brother's life is in danger, I have to do something about it now!"

"You're right, Susan. We'll go to the police right now," Roger said, hurrying to keep up with her.

Susan marched straight to her car. "No police. The caller warned me what would happen, remember? We can't take the chance. And now Andy Walker has seen us together. He must know that you're helping me." She slid in behind the wheel, and Roger climbed in on the passenger side.

"But how did Walker know you had the disk?" Roger wondered aloud.

"Good question," Susan said. Then her eyes widened. "What an *idiot* I am!" she shouted. "I just remembered where I first saw Andy! He was standing with some other people in the alley in back of HyperPlay. It was when you stopped to talk to that guard—remember?"

Roger gulped and nodded miserably. "He probably wondered why I was so interested."

"He might have written down your license plate number and traced the car," Susan said.

"I'll bet you're right. Then, when he

saw you working at HyperPlay—"

Susan looked grim as she skidded to a stop in front of her apartment building. "Hang on a minute," she said. "I have to go inside and get the disk."

A few minutes later, she returned, carrying the disk and a couple of flashlights. "The caller told me to drive to the city dump," she said in a shaky voice. "That's where I'm supposed to exchange the disk for Jay." She pulled onto the street. "Ironic, isn't it? This whole nightmare began in a dumpster, and now we're ending up at the dump!"

About 15 minutes later, they reached the end of the dirt road leading into the city dump. Ahead, they could see a half dozen very large dumpsters. She knew they were for recycled materials such as glass and newspapers. Just beyond the dumpsters was a vast wasteland of trash.

Susan and Roger automatically put their hands over their noses as they climbed out of the car. "Whew! This place sure smells bad," Susan muttered.

Then she heard noises that gave her the creeps. She knew that these scratchy, scuffling sounds could only be creatures like rats and cockroaches searching for food in the trash.

"Just where are you supposed to make the exchange?" Roger whispered.

"Don't turn around." The harsh voice came from behind them.

Susan froze. She noticed that the voice was very odd. It sounded like a woman trying to sound like a man!

"Okay, where's the disk? Hand it over!" the kidnapper demanded.

"Don't worry. I have it," Susan said. "But where's my brother?"

"Oh, no—first things first," the kidnapper insisted. "Come on, now. Hand over the disk."

Susan was frightened. She reached into her jacket pocket and pulled out the disk. At the same time, Roger yelled, "No! Don't give it up until—"

"*Shut up,*" the kidnapper growled.

Susan held the disk up over her head. Then, in the darkness, she heard someone moving toward her. Turning around, she quickly put her hand behind her back. "Stop! If you come near me, I swear that I'll toss this disk out into that sea of trash," Susan said in the toughest voice she could muster. "Now where's my brother?"

Then she squinted into the darkness, trying to get a good look at the kidnapper. But what she saw was a soft ray of moonlight glinting off the barrel of a gun.

Chapter 13

"The little creep's over there in the dumpster," the kidnapper snapped. "Now hand over the—"

"Roger!" Susan shouted. "Go over there and check on Jay!" She could hardly believe how angry her voice sounded. Inside, she was shaking.

"Don't move!" the kidnapper yelled. "I'm warning you—"

But Roger had already taken a quick step to one side. That widened the gap between him and Susan. Now the kidnapper swung the gun back and forth, frantically trying to cover them both.

"*Stop!*" The kidnapper's peculiar voice cried out. Now Susan was *certain* it was a woman.

"I can't believe it," Susan thought to herself. "So it's not Andy Walker after all. But if it's not him—"

Then she heard a groan coming from the dumpster. "Here!" she yelled at Roger, tossing the disk to him.

The kidnapper swung around to face Roger just as Susan dashed to the dumpster. There was her brother, lying bound and gagged. His head was on top of some damp old newspapers.

"You've got the kid. Now, give me the disk!" the kidnapper demanded. Susan heard Roger sigh. She knew he was trying to think fast.

Susan hurried to loosen the ropes and remove the gag from Jay's mouth. Then the boy sat up. His face looked white and frightened in the moonlight.

"Are you all right?" she asked, as she helped him out of the dumpster. Jay nodded, his whole body trembling.

Roger had delayed as long as he could. "Okay, here's the disk. Take it!"

he snapped at the kidnapper.

But at just that moment, they heard the sound of sirens in the distance. The kidnapper howled in fury.

Susan pushed Jay behind the dumpster just as the kidnapper swung around. Then, hearing the crack of gunfire, she threw herself to the ground.

Then the beams of several pairs of headlights pierced the darkness. The first patrol car skidded to a stop next to the dumpsters.

The kidnapper tried to fire again, but the gun jammed. Susan saw the woman toss the gun to the side as she turned and raced into the sea of trash.

Susan went after her. Later, she couldn't figure out just what had made her do it. Likely, it was pure frustration and anger. But she quickly closed the distance between them and then dove at the kidnapper, knocking her off her feet.

A moment later, the police officers found Susan sitting on top of the kidnapper. Her clothes were filthy, and she smelled like the inside of a trashcan. But her smile of triumph was dazzling!

*   *   *

The next morning, as Susan was pouring orange juice, there was a knock on the door. It was Roger. "I just talked to the cops," he told her. "You'll never believe who they arrested."

Susan shrugged. "At first I was sure it was Andy. But then, at the dump, I realized it had to be either Jane or Patricia. But I haven't been able to figure out why Andy had the virus program on *his* computer if—"

"It was all three of them," Roger said with a grin. "They all had their own reasons to hurt the company. So they got together and came up with the virus scheme. Then the disk Jay found got thrown out by accident.

"They panicked. They had to get it back before someone figured out what they were up to. So the three of them worked together as a team to kidnap Jay—and then to give each other alibis. Good thing their plan backfired."

"How did the cops know to come to the dump?" Susan asked.

Roger made a little bow. "While you were up here getting the infected disk, I called the cops on my cell phone." He grinned as he took a seat and reached for a glass of orange juice. "You were really *something* last night, Susan! I'm impressed. I had no idea you were such a fighter!"

"Yeah!" Jay exclaimed. "You're a champion, Sue! You saved everyone. But, hey—I'm hungry. Are you going to fix breakfast pretty soon?"

"No," Susan said as she took a seat, leaned back, and crossed her arms. "You guys are! Don't you know the rule about champions? They don't have to cook breakfast!"

COMPREHENSION QUESTIONS

RECALL

1. Why did Susan Hoskins have custody of her younger brother?

2. Where did Susan and Roger meet the kidnapper?

3. Why were Jay and Buddy in trouble with the police?

IDENTIFYING CHARACTERS

1. Which character got a temporary job at HyperPlay?

2. Which character warned Jay about illegal dumpster diving?

3. Which character caught Susan staring at his computer screen?

DRAWING CONCLUSIONS

1. When Susan learned that Jay had been kidnapped, why didn't she call the police?

2. Why did Susan think it might have been a mistake to introduce Roger to her brother?

3. Why did Jay's computer crash when he tried to play *Lion of Doom*?

VOCABULARY

1. Jay said that he and Buddy "got into some *rank* places." What does *rank* mean?

2. Patricia Leong was suspected of passing company secrets to a *rival*. What's a *rival*?

3. Susan accidentally hit the *mouse* on Andy Walker's desk. What's a *mouse*?